MRS. EVERYBODY

THREE WIVES THREE HUSBANDS

TENA SELDAN

plicit Press

CHAPTER 1

BEING MARRIED to an *Elvis* impersonator was not how Dominique thought she'd be tying the knot. Fifth in line, standing next to her soon-to-be-husband, Raul, she shifted from foot to foot, looking as nervous as she was. Her nerves had nothing to do with getting married, mind you, and everything to do with how she was getting married.

"We don't have to do this..." Raul said.

"Oh no, we really do!" She tried to compose herself, to give the illusion of calm, even though she was dangerously close to throwing up.

Rachel, another *almost-bride,* touched Dominique on her shoulder, motioning with her eyes that perhaps they should go outside for some air. She signaled, again with her eyes, for Reed, her own *almost-groom,* to keep Raul company. As she and Dominique exited into the warm Vegas night, both women suddenly felt free.

"Need a minute, huh?" Another bride-to-be was standing outside, smoking a cigarette. Sophie looked like she was getting married, dressed, veil, everything.

"I'm Rachel, this is Dominique. Are you done already?"

"I'm Sophie... No! My guy's gone to try and find rings. He had one job, *one*. Is this the way it's going to be? Marriage?"

"It gets worse!" Dominique laughed, relaxing a little bit, it seemed.

"Well, Jeb is off to a great start... Got me all dressed up and out here waiting for *Elvis*, with no rings!" Sophie said.

"Is that his name? My grown-up juvenile is called Reed," Rachel said!

"Raul," Dominique said, raising her hand unnecessarily.

Sophie offered them a cigarette, Rachel taking one, Dominique not, even though she looked like she needed one. As she held her lighter up to Rachel, Sophie looked over the two women, greatly underdressed for the most important day of their lives. One wore a light cream jump-suit, the other a pair of slacks, and what really was just a tank top. It was all white, yes, but Rachel still looked like she had just come off a shift at a local bar.

"You look really pretty," Dominique said to Sophie before taking the cigarette from Rachel and dragging hard. "He doesn't like me smoking," she said, giving an explanation they hadn't asked for.

"$125, down the road..." Sophie said.

"Cheaper than the cost of the wedding? Well done you!" Rachel wasn't being sarcastic. She just sounded that way.

"I need a drink," Dominique said, handing the cigarette back to Rachel.

"I need a few..." Rachel whispered, dropping the smoked out cig on the ground.

"Found them," they heard someone say through the dark *daylight* of the Vegas strip. Jeb came up running, quickly, a box in hand, holding it up as if to prove the success of his ring-finding mission.

"I hope it fits," Sophie said, irritated suddenly. "Jeb, Dominique...and Rachel. They're also getting hitched here tonight, although, we've been thinking, and we might just disappear into the night and leave the three of you to marry each other.

Jeb greeted the two women, and then looked around for the two missing members of '*you three!*' He could really use some more testosterone now, feeling more than a little attacked by all three females.

"I think we'd better go inside," Dominique said, apparently calm now and having resigned herself to how her wedding day would play out.

"Yeah... Let's get this over with..." Sophie said, pulling Jeb into the tiny chapel by his hand, although she might as well have been pulling him by his nose.

Dominique was putting on her bravest face, now. She mumbled something in Spanish, which confirmed her accent for everyone, even though they had no clue what she was saying. She walked up to Raul and introduced him to everybody. The men shook hands, Reed and Raul kissed the women they hadn't met yet on the cheek, and then every couple stood silently, watching the newlyweds exit one by one, looking happier than the three pairs of them combined.

Sophie was the first to wed, followed by Rachel. Dominique needed a minute, so two couples went before Raul and herself. But then she was married, relieved that Sophie and Rachel stayed to support her, witnessing her nuptials, impromptu guests at the wedding they all thought wouldn't happen, actually.

When they all stood outside on the sidewalk, the three men looked relieved. The women seemed anxious still so that everyone was suddenly curious about every other person's backstory. Vegas was supposed to be fun and carefree. The whole city seemed to be designed for pleasure. But Rachel, Dominique, and Sophie looked like they had just been sentenced to life.

Looking at these three women, you would have thought that they should be the happiest females in the world. They were all young, early twenties, all three of them incredibly beautiful in different but exceptionally obvious ways. Their husbands too were gorgeous, all three of them tall and strapping, also in their twenties.

As far as couples went, they all looked perfect together. Even if you swopped them around though, they would still look exceptionally good together. Dominique and Raul were exotic, Spanish, natural tans that made both the other women envious.

Rachel and Reed were typical South, from Savannah, and they spoke with that overly polite drawl that made you think they'd come from good homes. This made the others even more curious, all of them wondering if they'd been raised so well, why were they getting married shotgun style in Vegas?

Sophie and Jeb seemed the most worldly. A New York couple choosing to marry in Vegas was another point of interest, again making the group curious. They all just wanted to sit down now and have a conversation that would clear up the confusion all of them had at these people they had met just an hour before.

The women walked in front, Sophie center, looking like the only bride. They walked a ways down the strip, having a conversation that seemed to border on collusion. Sophie turned suddenly to face the three men, speaking for the group.

"We've decided that we'd like to go to *Italy* for our

honeymoon," she said, looking at all three men square in the face.

The men looked confused until all three women pointed to the Venetian hotel across the road. Raul, Reed, and Jeb all held their pockets, fingers over their wallets as they realized that they really had no choice!

CHAPTER 2

THE COUPLES CHECKED into one of the plush penthouse suites at the mock-Italian Venetian a little after 11. The men decided on the one room because splitting it three ways was doable and because the women seemed to have bonded, and by the look of things, it would just be safer to keep them together.

"Anybody hungry?" Raul asked, looking at the room service menu, reading out the items slowly, like he was just learning to speak English.

"I'm going to shower," Rachel said.

"Anything's fine," said Dominique, pulling Sophie to the bathroom so that all three women were now in the excessively proportioned bathroom, with just Sophie's cosmetics bag and Rachel's overnight. They were really ill-prepared, separately, for an overnight stay anywhere, but together, all supplies combined, they would be just fine.

Reed took another menu off the coffee table and started to make some suggestions. Raul had a few ideas of his own, Jeb quiet.

"Are you sure you don't want to wait for them?" he asked.

"Probably safer, yeah... But they did say anything, right?" Reed was really hungry.

"No... Dominique said anything. And anything is never anything with that one..." Raul wasn't throwing his wife under the bus as much as he was just stating the obvious.

"Who knows how long they're gonna be. And anyway, we'll get them some chocolate, strawberries, and champagne. That should make this feel like their wedding night right?" Reed was already calling down for room service, his stomach making its emptiness obvious.

"So, are you from Spain, or Latin America," Jeb asked Raul as Reed placed the order. Quite a matter of factly, Raul summarized his short life in three sentences. 'He and Dominique met in Madrid a few months ago. She was an American citizen, he wasn't. They rushed to get married because he was being deported in a few days!'

"That's no guarantee that you'll be allowed to stay..." Jeb was equally matter of fact.

"Yeah, but with a woman like Dominique, I really hope you do!" Reed had finished on the phone.

"She is something..." Raul said.

"A little more than something, my man... She's everything!" Reed wasn't sure if he had crossed a line.

"You're wife is beautiful too, both your wives!" Raul passed both men an honest compliment.

They talked a bit about their new brides, how they met, and what attracted them to each other. But, as men do, they talked mostly about the secret bedroom skills their women had, skills they felt free to discuss with each other because this was as far as it would go.

All three kept their eyes on the bathroom door and

spoke in hushed whispers, not wanting their blatant objecti-
fication heard. The beers from the minibar made them relax
a little more, and as they sipped and spoke, they all realized
that it had, in fact, been quite an eventful day. It was good to
just relax, no pressure, and shoot the breeze, even if
shooting the breeze meant revealing intimate details about
their wives.

In the time that it took for the food to arrive, about 30
minutes, the details passed between them did more than
just make the wait bearable. Jeb, for example, explained in
explicit detail that Sophie's mouth wasn't just good for talk-
ing. He tried to explain her mouth skills as best he could,
but even with the incredible amount of detail, it was clear to
the others that this was something you had to experience.

Rachel, according to Reed, had a way of making him
very *lazy*. She liked to do all the work, and she was very
good at doing everything. She had an understanding of her
body, and how it worked, and she had as intimate a knowledge of what a man wanted, and how to give it to him. He
knew that it was just him, too, since he was really the only
person that Rachel had ever slept with.

According to Raul, he fell in love with Dominique's
body before he fell in love with her. He couldn't pinpoint
one single thing that she did, but the way he described her
body made the other two sit up and lean in, paying more
attention than should have been cool, what with the woman
being spoken about being the wife of the man doing the
speaking. They had all seen her body, of course, at least the
outline of it in the cream jumpsuit, and so it was easy for
them to believe everything being told to them in a thick
Spanish accent!

"Damn!" Jeb said.

"Yeah... Wow!" Reed stood up and went to the door, the

room service arriving just as Raul finished his regaling. Just before he opened the door, he noticed a slight bulge in his pants. He put his hand down his pants and positioned his semi-hardness so that he didn't look like a man about to get some. As he let the waiter into the suite, he noticed Jeb shifting on the sofa too, making the *worst kept secret* of his own arousal.

Raul noticed this, of course. He looked at the bathroom door, thinking that he must really have done good, to be able to call Dominique his wife. He knew too that she was in love with him, only him, and so he knew that even if the two men lusted after her, as many men did, she was all his, *to have and to hold,* forever and ever.

"Food's here," Reed said, knocking on the bathroom door. No response came, but none of them were worried. One woman in a bathroom was not to be disturbed. When a group of them gathered in what to them was holy ground, disturbing them was done only if you had a death wish.

Jeb filled a plate with a savory variety from the meaty basket and took the food and his beer out onto the balcony. He needed air, and also needed a distraction from his unyielding arousal. Reed was quickly morphing to full arousal too, Raul's voice still lingering in his head. He sat down and tackled the food, hoping too that his *too huge to hide problem* would dissipate soon.

"It's beautiful here," Raul said, joining Jeb on the balcony.

"Lights have a way of creating magic, no doubt. But come morning, the harshness of the city comes to light, unable to hide itself from the sun..."

"Very poetic, my friend," Raul said, coming up beside Jeb against the railing.

"Yeah... I just wish I'd given her a better wedding, you know?" Jeb was a little down.

"The night is still young..." Raul brought his bottle to Jeb's, clanking the bottles against each other just a little too hard.

CHAPTER 3

THE BATHROOM DOOR OPENED, and the three women exited, looking every bit like the promise of a good time. Dominique had nothing but a towel wrapped around her, Rachel and Sophie's clean underwear, and sexy black and grey ensembles that looked like they had been purchased together. Self-conscious they were not, keenly aware of their good looks, and also just comfortable in the knowledge that they were amongst friends.

Raul and Jeb walked in off the balcony, and both went straight for their wives. Rachel was already seated on Reed's lap, eating a rather large strawberry. Jeb put a mini-sausage roll in Sophie's mouth, and Raul was looking at his almost naked wife as she finished his beer.

"You look, nice," he said, to Dominique, to everybody.

"I have no clothing," Dominique said, pulling him in for a kiss.

"I'm not complaining," Reed said, before realizing he shouldn't have said it.

"Neither are we," Rachel said, smiling at Dominique,

winking at her husband. There seemed to be a playfulness between them that was a secret that only they knew.

Sophie came up to Rachel and took a huge bite out of her strawberry. Rachel dipped the remainder of the large fruit in the chocolate fondue and put the whole thing in Sophie's mouth. Then the two women kissed the air between them.

"This game you're playing is very dangerous..." Raul said, kissing the side of his wife's face, but speaking to Rachel and Sophie.

"What game?" Sophie asked, running her fingers through Reed's hair, pulling her own husband in for a kiss. Reed looked at Rachel, then at Dominique, despite his best efforts not to look. Raul caught him looking, and played with the top of her towel, mimicking its removal.

"I think we're all just tired, or..." Reed was saying.

"Horny," Raul said, looking from one man to the other.

There was just one bedroom in the penthouse, and the open-plan living room. So if they were to act on their arousal, then a couple would take the bedroom, another the living room. And the third couple would have to take a walk and come back later. This was suddenly at a top of all the women's minds, as they tried to think how consummation of their wedding night might be possible.

"Well there isn't much we can do about that, now is there," Rachel said, Sophie echoing.

"Isn't there?" Raul asked, pouring champagne for the ladies.

"Yes, isn't there?" Jeb asked his eyes on Dominique.

"Well taking it in shifts is not my idea of romance..." Sophie said, voicing verbatim what Rachel was just thinking!

"Who said anything about shifts," Raul said, picking his

wife up carefully so that she didn't spill her champagne, and carrying her to the balcony.

He pressed himself up against her and kissed her on her forehead before connecting with her mouth. He let her towel drop to the ground, shielding her nakedness with his imposing frame. The passion of his lips on hers was rivaled only by the passionate movement of his fingers up and down her back, and on her backside.

Dominique unzipped his pants, sending her delicate fingers down them and onto where her husband was firming up quite quickly. His largeness made it necessary for her to unbutton his pants before returning her hand to where he was now completely engorged. She moved her fingers up and down on him, base to tip, tip to base, as he moved his own fingers between her legs.

The others were watching, closely. Raul and Jeb were fully erect too now, wanting desperately to be free of their pants. They both looked from their wives to Raul, who now had a finger deep in his wife, their eyes locked. Sophie and Rachel sipped on their champagne, paying no attention to their husbands, completely mesmerized by the scene playing out on the balcony just a little way away.

"Wow," Reed said, too loud. Rachel looked at him, before looking at Jeb, who was also uttering a series of audible 'wows!'

Then Rachel and Sophie were on their husbands. They went to work on their pants, completely removing them. They straddled their men, kissing them on the mouth, on the neck, on the chest. They pressed their underwear against each other, bringing their husbands to full attention now, increasing immensely their need to be attended to. Sophie and Rachel pressed themselves harder against them, not sure how to proceed, even though Dominique and Raul had really set the tone for a 'what happens in vegas' type situation.

Raul was really going into his wife now, two and then three fingers. Then he was on his knees, putting his lips on hers, licking, and then sucking the sweet flow. Then he was again pulling on her lips with his, before gently holding her open and sending his tongue into her waiting wetness.

Jeb was the first to see Dominique's spectacular chest. She was pulling on her ample breasts, parting them, and then pushing them together. Then she was pressing them hard into her chest before pulling provocatively on her nipples. She too watched Jeb, watching her. The attention fuelled something inside her because her movements on herself became almost theatrical. She was performing for him.

Not just him,too, because Reed was also watching her now. His eyes moved from the balcony to Jeb, and then quickly back to the balcony. He was dripping into the cotton of his briefs, partly because of his wife, moving on him in suggestive gyrations, partly, if not mostly because of Dominique, who was now gripping Raul's head as he drove his tongue inside her.

Dominique's eyes were now closed, as Raul expertly brought her closer and closer. She was panting loudly so that both couples were now looking at her with intense curiosity. They had never, between the four of them, been a part of anything like this before, but as Dominique made vocal her incredible eruption, they were suddenly all primed for whatever this night was going to be!

"The couple that plays together, right?" Reed said, pulling his underwear off completely, surrendering all inhibition now, and giving himself completely to this night that he would never have had the balls to initiate...

CHAPTER 4

RACHEL HAD ALSO DECIDED that they were too far in it to retreat now, and so she positioned herself between Reed's legs. She went to work on him, much to his relief. The whole room disappeared now, as Reed disappeared into Rachel's mouth.

Not to be outdone, Sophie pulled her husband's undies off. She teased him with just her lips, and then her tongue. Then she too was playing now you see me now you don't with his penis. Jeb held her head, moving it up and down on himself the way he liked to do even though this was completely unnecessary.

Raul and Dominique walked in, proud of what they had done. While Raul poured more drinks, Dominique made quick work of the women's bras. She then helped them out of their panties, evening the playing field. She took a glass from her husband and watched him as he put the tray on the coffee table. He really was attractive!

Raul seemed to be the most caring, or the most confident because he was kissing Rachel up and down her back, his eyes on Reed. The men seemed to make an unspoken gentlemen's agreement, because Raul was soon on his knees behind Rachel, biting gently into her buttocks. She was shocked briefly and looked at Reed, who winked at her, so that she relaxed into it.

Jeb was looking at Dominique now, who again had found her own breasts with her own fingers. She was an incredible temptress, Jeb torn between the woman working him over *like a boss*, and the incredible urge to reach for, and touch, Dominique!

The temptress made the decision for him. She walked over and got beside Sophie. She took Sophie's hair in her hand and pulled lightly, lifting the mouth from the meat. Then she put her hand flat on the back of Sophie's head and pushed down as slowly. She repeated this a few times, Sophie going with it, enjoying what she was doing to her husband, and secretly thrilled by the addition of this exotic beauty.

Dominique reached for Jeb, taking his hand and guiding it onto her breast. He was finding it hard to breathe now, the effort audible. Dominique just smiled, guiding the same hand over to the other one.

Sophie side-eyed Dominique now, and lifted her mouth off Jeb. She moved so that Dominique could take her place between his legs, while she got up on the sofa and fed herself to her husband. Jeb jerked into her, onto her, as Dominique made contact with his thick, hard meat, and as he disappeared into this new mouth, he mouthed his appreciation into his wife's pulsating tunnel, which smelled and tasted like home. He devoured her with every part of his mouth, too, while Dominique used every part of her own mouth on his manhood.

Reed was watching Dominique at work, and he was incredibly envious. He didn't even notice that Raul was now licking his wife directly on her *happiness* and that Rachel was enjoying every single one of his expert licks. She didn't skip a beat on his meat mind you, so he really had nothing to be worried about, except for the fact that Raul was enjoying this more than Rachel, it seemed.

Then Raul was biting her butt again, kissing her lower back. His hands moved over her beautiful rear, parting her cheeks and then pushing them together, pulling them apart to reveal her beautiful bud, before hiding it again with her cheeks. When again he had parted the *Red Sea*, he place just the tip of his tongue on the perfect bud and started to lick small circles onto it.

Rachel's back arched, lifting her mouth of Reed, which returned his attention to his wife. Their eyes met as she returned her lips to his shaft, and she had a look that said what was happening behind her was very, very nice. Reed smiled, still unsure how they had gotten here, but very glad that they had.

Jeb came close, and then he wasn't. Then again he was incredibly close, only to have his orgasm pass him by, although only just. Dominique really had a skill with her mouth that rivaled Sophie's, but this was no time to play comparisons. Instead, Jeb grabbed his wife's round behind and pushed her into his mouth just a little more. He was eating her out with the reckless abandon of adolescence.

Sophie grabbed Jeb's head now. She was incredibly close, and there really was no turning back. She hadn't known to what extent Dominique climaxing on the balcony had impacted her, this impact now rippling over her in her own version of this beautiful end. Her flow filled Jeb's mouth so that for the moment he forgot even the mouth on him. He squeezed her cheeks tighter, pulled her closer, and sent his tongue deeper, sealing this with his lips tightly against his wife's.

She wasn't as loud as Dominique. Jeb didn't expect her to be, her body communicating everything he needed to know. He kept them locked in this hold for as long as it took for her to recover. When she had, somewhat, she came down face to face and sucked the taste of herself from his wet mouth.

Raul was licking both Rachel's holes now, wanting to be inside her, but nervous suddenly, aware that there must be rules if this play was to yield pleasure dividends. He moved his tongue over her and then inside her, as she mimicked with her own tongue on Reed what was being done to her. She felt her own orgasm somewhere in the distance, but it seemed to be waving at her from so far away that she decided to put all her focus and energy into drawing liquid from her husband.

Reed grabbed her head and held her on himself, thrusting hard into her face as he went over the edge into a bliss he hadn't expected at all tonight. He wondered, as he emptied himself into her mouth, if Raul had known this would happen. He wondered if the freaky foreigner had somehow planned it.

If so, he high-fived him in his head, his eyes on Dominique again as she swallowed every last drop erupting from Jeb now!

CHAPTER 5

RAUL AND RACHEL were the only two yet to experience the thrill of climax. The two were in no hurry, though, it seemed, Raul getting up to get more drinks and Rachel rinsing her mouth with champagne.

"That was interesting," Jeb said, running his fingers up and down Sophie's arm.

"Yes, it was," Reed said, wrapping a towel around himself as he walked out the bathroom following his post-climax pee. The others, all comfortably naked, gave him a look.

He ignored these stares, taking a strawberry, dipping it into the chocolate, and then putting the whole thing in his mouth. He was moving his fingers over Rachel, and it felt nice. But it was obvious that he was still basking in the glory of his own recent explosion, so his intentions weren't clear.

She let him touch her, her eyes on Raul though, who was now kissing his wife. She felt lacking, slightly, as though she was not attractive enough to bring Raul to orgasm until their eyes met again. The look on his face said everything his mouth couldn't, and so she relaxed, knowing that, tonight at least, all good things would certainly come to those who waited.

Again it was Dominique and Raul blazing the trail. He had pulled the coffee table off the rug, replaced it with his wife, and come down on the floor beside her. That he was aroused was not in question, his massive erection pulsing from side to side in front of him as he moved his fingers all over Dominique's body. He was kissing her neck now as his fingers traced circles on her thighs. Then he was pulling on her nipples between his teeth as soon as his fingers found her lower lips.

He wasn't urgent with his devouring this time, already having brought Dominique over. Her body relaxed knowing that he would really take his time now, savoring every possible moment.

Raul's mouth found her breasts again. Slowly, tenderly, he bit into them, before sucking on them sensually. His hand was moving up and down on her legs, the other providing the support needed to hold them up.

Jeb and Sophie were also getting hot and heavy on the sofa. His fingers moved inside her as they lay side by side on the sofa. Both their eyes were on the couple on the rug, who seemed suddenly to forget that there was anybody else in the world.

Raul turned Dominique over and brought her to her knees. He came up behind her and positioned himself almost underneath her. He found her entrance quickly, going all the way up inside her. It seemed to be happening in slow motion for those observing, even though the entry was a little swift for Raul.

He suddenly felt an urgent need to be inside her. His eyes on Rachel made him fully aware of how much he wanted to explore her, but knowing that he couldn't take his time with her. He had, literally, his whole life with Dominique, but Rachel, tonight was it. So he needed to relieve the tension that had started to build in him when he was nibbling on her behind as she brought Reed to climax.

As Raul thrust steadily into Dominique, he didn't, not for a second, take his eyes off Rachel. Rachel's own eyes went to Sophie, suddenly uncomfortable by Raul's incessant stare. She watched as Jeb mounted his own wife, clearly taking his cues from the Spaniard.

Dominique and Sophie were on their way, quite swiftly, to their second orgasms. Rachel wasn't jealous, but she did wonder why Reed was suddenly so inattentive. Then, of course, she remembered that they had never done this before, so it really wasn't fair of her to expect that he knew what to do.

She took a deep breath and guided Reed's hands over every part of her as she brought them down onto the rug next to Dominique and Raul. Then she was kissing him on his mouth, positioning herself underneath him. He slid into her easily, guided by Rachel's intimate understanding of her own body.

Raul pushed Dominique down now so that she was lying flat on her stomach. His face was now next to Rachel's, his hardness inside Dominique, Reed's inside his wife. She pulled her mouth off Reed and turned a bit so that her mouth connected with Raul's. The whole room seemed to breathe a sigh of relief now.

Their kissing was passionate, almost too much. Raul really loved the taste of Rachel, the feel of her lips, and how her tongue moved across his. He also enjoyed the familiarity of his wife, whose skill was unquestionable, but the thought of Rachel lingered heavily on his mind. He really could think of nothing else now.

Rachel loved the feeling of her husband too, but she'd be lying if she didn't admit, to herself at least, that Raul's mouth intensified this sensation on her now. It felt more complete, somehow, in ways that she couldn't explain to herself.

Dominique was caught up in her bliss now, taken there swiftly and skillfully by her husband's mastery. Rachel watched him move on her, from her face-to-face vantage point. It really was quite something to behold.

So caught up was she, in fact, by this feast for the eyes, that she didn't even notice her own husband spilling over into his version of ecstasy. Reed spilled over into her with short, sharp thrusts. But even this quickness, or the intensity of it, wasn't enough to distract her.

When he pulled out of her he borrowed for his wife's mouth, briefly. Then he stood up and went to the bathroom, again needing to pee. Raul pulled out of his wife too, having also brought her and himself to a magnificent finish. Rachel was the only one yet to experience what the other women had now experienced twice.

This sort of bothered her, and it didn't. She was patient, and she knew by the way he was looking at her that she just needed to give Raul a minute to recover.

CHAPTER 6

RAUL STOOD NEXT TO REED, who was still peeing. He really flowed post-climax. Raul also emptied himself into the elegant toilet bowl, watching his stream, his mind racing.

"Would it be okay with you if I..." he asked, not looking at Reed.

"Huh?"

"You know..." He made a gesture with his hand that made his question obvious, but a little inappropriate.

"With who, my wife?" Reed asked, mock surprise.

"I'm sorry, I just thought I'd ask..." Raul was now shaking the last drops from himself.

"I'm just messing with you, buddy. If she's cool, I'm cool. Can I..." Reed repeated Raul's gesture.

"I know you want to... And I know Dominique, she wants to. So go for it!"

When they exited the bathroom, they were a little surprised to find Jeb on the rug, lying on his back, the three women attending to various parts of him. Dominique was sitting on his face, her mouth on his nipples. Sophie was moving her own mouth up and down on his shaft and Rachel, she was licking his balls like they were made of *sugar and spice and everything nice.*

Reed and Raul, rethinking their plan, got themselves beers and sat down on the sofa, a meaty basket between them. Sophie really was good at what she was doing, and so she made for a good show. Raul's eyes were on Rachel mostly, though, scanning her body as she writhed and arched on the rug, looking like she was moving through the water, her tongue not once leaving Jeb's nuts.

Jeb couldn't look at the two men. He couldn't speak, his mouth occupied. Dominique was grinding herself against his lips. Her teeth were biting into his nipples hard now, as his own teeth devoured her lips. They were locked in a sensual feast of one another's most sensitive body parts, and so nothing existed around them. Rachel and Sophie's bodies now rubbed up against each other as they were now both between Jeb's legs, both their tongues on his testicles.

Dominique leaned further down and took Jeb into her mouth, her wet place still moving over his mouth. He was sucking hard now, enjoying the thrill of the three pairs of lips on him. Reed and Raul were hard again, thrilled by what they were witnessing. Reed really wanted to lift Dominique off Jeb's face, but courtesy meant that he would have to wait for his turn. Raul watched Rachel more intensely now, also wanting to lift her off the ground, but not sure if the time was right.

Jeb's legs parted further, his knees bending. Dominique lifted herself off his face, repositioning herself so that her new seat was his stomach. Rachel and Sophie moved out of the way, what was about to happen was now clear to both of them. Rachel's eyes locked with Raul's, and he started to move toward her. He was quickly intercepted by Sophie, though, armed with a chocolate-covered strawberry.

She pushed him back down on the sofa, feeding him the fruit as she straddled him. Rachel took the drink in Reed's hand and sipped it as she made her way to the bathroom. It was clearly a free for all tonight, but it was also definitely a case of first come first served. She decided to get into the shower, to pass the time, and wait for the chance she wasn't even sure she would get now.

Sophie worked Raul's hardness inside herself quickly. Her chest rubbed against his as she moved up and down on him, excitedly. Raul really wanted her mouth on him but it was clear the parts of him she wanted. He could not deny the splendor, though, and soon enough he was sitting back on the sofa watching Sophie work herself mostly into various stages of ecstasy.

Reed watched Dominique do the same to Jeb. He moved to the floor, wanting desperately to get his hands at least on the Spanish beauty now riding Jeb into a daze. He touched her back, lightly, moved his fingers down to her too-perfect butt, rested, and then sunk his fingers into the succulence.

Then his mouth was on her skin, soft kisses tracing up and down her back as Dominique moved deliberately slowly on Jeb. She had all of him inside her now, and she had such control over him that he could do nothing but watch. His eyes met Reed's and begged him not to disturb her. Reed had no intention to, but he really wanted a throbbing part of him inside her too.

Reed stood up, over Jeb now, giving Dominique's mouth access to himself. Without missing a turn on Jeb she swallowed the full length of the man whose nuts dangled above Jeb's face. Jeb didn't mind. Actually, he didn't even notice.

His view of Dominique's rodeo on him was not in the least obstructed.

Raul was now on his back across the sofa. Sophie, still on top of him, his full mast in her sensuous sea, was moving quickly back and forth. Then as quickly she was moving side to side, before resuming her backward and forwards which was essentially an up and down. She was as excited as she was excitable, and Raul resisted the urge to tell her to slow down, knowing that she was obviously just doing what she needed to be doing, what she thought he wanted her to be doing.

His eyes went to the bathroom door, slightly ajar. He caught Rachel just as she slipped back inside, having come out to get a bottle of champagne. He really wanted Sophie to be done on him now, not because it wasn't fun, but because his full focus was on Rachel. He couldn't think what it was about her, perhaps it was everything. But all of him really, really wanted a taste of all of her.

Sophie's movement on him sped up somewhat and he thought she might be close. But then she slowed down, pulling his hands onto her perky breasts and squeezing. Then she picked up the pace again, before once again slowing down, enjoying the fullness of his penetration. Raul knew that there was nothing that he could do until Sophie was done.

Dominique had already succeeded in bringing an epic orgasm from Jeb. He was still inside her but obviously spent. She moved in slow circles on him, easing him down from his euphoria, Reed still in her mouth, watching her, waiting for her to dismount. She pulled her face off Reed, eased herself off Jeb, and lay facedown on the rug. Then she looked up at Reed in a way that said 'what are you waiting for...'

CHAPTER 7

REED COULDN'T BELIEVE that the time had come, at last. He looked up at Raul, who wasn't looking at him, his attention fully on Sophie, who was moving on him with renewed vigor now, kissing her husband. Jeb had stood up now and made his way to the sofa. He seemed too excited by what was going on.

Dominique raised her rear slightly, inviting Reed to take her. He was breathing slowly, trying to focus himself, not wanting to seem too eager. He had waited a minute for this moment, but now that it was upon him, he was suddenly unsure of himself.

He looked at himself. He was hard as hell, but this wasn't what he was checking. He knew that he wasn't small. He wasn't. But he wasn't as thick as Jeb, or as long and thick as Raul. This was no time to play comparisons or doubt himself. 'Motion in the ocean,' he repeated to himself, over and over again, as he positioned himself on top of Dominique, who seemed almost hungry for him now.

His hands grabbed the parts of her she was literally feeding him. He squeezed, gently at first, and then with a firmness that made her rise a little more into his grip. He moved one hand down her back and then underneath her, lifting her off the floor. Her back to his front now, he pressed against her and exhaled loudly. Again he was looking at Raul, who again was not looking at him.

Dominique tilted her head back and kissed his chin, bringing his attention fully to the now. Reed kissed her on the mouth, present, pressing himself just that much harder against her ample behind. It felt like he thought it would. It felt much better actually. Steadily, still a little unsure of himself, he started to thrust against her, snuggly sandwiched between her cheeks.

The kiss sent sparks all over his face, and he pulled away briefly, shocked by the intensity. Then their lips were locked again, and the electricity fused their faces together. His hand, carefully on her hip, pulled her back as he moved forward, then pushed her forward slightly as he prepared for another delicious delivery against her.

His other hand found the ampleness of her breasts, and he was transfixed. He started briefly to play the comparison game again, between Rachel and Dominique this time, but quickly stopped himself. He knew that she was not his to have, and he loved that Rachel actually let him have this. He really loved Rachel, he knew, and so this was purely physical.

After making a mental note to find a spectacular way to thank Rachel for this wedding present, he centered himself and brought full focus to the task at hand. This experience had nothing to do with Dominique now, but he had to make sure that she enjoyed it too. She played as big a role as his own carnal pleasure, and he knew that if he didn't do Dominique right, he wouldn't feel like this one-time experience was worth it. Reed was determined to make it count.

He eased them down again so that he was on top of her. She parted her legs and bent her knees, grinding against him hard. She wanted him inside her, and she was not going to wait much longer. Reed found her entrance and glided into her moist tightness with ease made possible by the incredible amount she was flowing. Dominique really was incredibly wet.

Reed went all the way in, and then pulled himself all the way out. Quickly he was all in again, and then all the way out. Each time he exited, she moaned and mumbled in Spanish. This turned him on even more, and then he was inside her again. But then he was out, and again the Spanish fell from her lips in sensuous whispers.

His hands moved to her hips now and he gripped hard, pushing her back into the rug with just his thumbs as his other fingers lifted her into himself. Then he sent himself into her completely and stayed. They both seemed to exhale together now, and as he started to thrust fully into her, no exit this time, she put her head on the rug and relaxed into what she knew was Reed's *taking* of her.

He took her completely, no change in position, no change of pace. She felt like all his imaginings, and then some, and the sounds coming from her let him know that he was getting it right. So he just kept doing what he was doing, no need for variation, until Dominique was once again loudly making the room aware that she had just gone over, again!

How it was that three couples with sexual appetites on par with one another was something none of them knew. Nobody could finger how they had all hit the wedding night jackpot, despite how they all found themselves in a Vegas hotel room having just said I do in a Vegas chapel. But it had happened. It was happening, and as Reed spilled his ecstasy into Dominique, he, for one, was very, very glad that it had!

He was glad a lot, tonight!

Sophie fell into Jeb's arms now, too, spent by her almost athletic fete on Raul, who hadn't had an orgasm, deliberately, saving himself for the woman who still hadn't come out of the bathroom.

CHAPTER 8

"WOW," Dominique said, to no one in particular.

"Yup," Jeb said, pulling Sophie onto him as he reclined on the sofa.

Raul got up and pulled a chilled bottle of champagne from an ice bucket, pouring everyone a glass. They brought their glasses to each other and then sipped a very necessary sip. Reed winked at Raul and then looked towards the bathroom. Raul nodded, not sure what he was going to do with Rachel yet, but knowing that this was definitely what he had waited for from the moment he knew this night would go this way.

He walked naked out onto the balcony, though, needing to get his head together. He needed to get a game plan in his head and found himself going to the conversation they had when the women were in the bathroom. Reed had said that Rachel made him lazy. He said that she had a way of doing, and enjoying, all the work. Perhaps this is what he had wanted. Perhaps this was what appealed to him, Dominique always expecting full participation.

If it was though, this wasn't the case now. He wanted to

do things to Rachel, with her and for her, that would blow her mind. He wanted her to experience being made love to, and to enjoy it, almost as much as she seemed to enjoy being the one in control. He hadn't figured out how, yet, though, so he just stood against the railing and breathed in the Vegas night.

"You scared?" Reed said, punching him on his shoulder.

"Nervous..." Raul said, honestly.

"I'm sure she wants to, too. If she didn't, we wouldn't be here, and I wouldn't have had the opportunity to experience what I just have!"

"Was it good?" Raul asked, looking at where his wife was still lying on the rug.

"You're one lucky, lucky man..." Reed said.

"I know!"

"Now, go, go and see why I too, am a very, very happy man!" Reed said, looking towards the bathroom again.

Raul breathed deep and looked at the bathroom door. "In a minute," he said.

Reed went inside and went straight to the fondue. He dipped a strawberry in it, excessively, and moved this still-dripping fruit over to Sophie, letting the chocolate drizzle onto her breasts. This excited Jeb, which excited Dominique. The four of them were suddenly drizzling chocolate onto each other, feeding each other fruit, their mouths moving across bodies tired but aroused.

Raul watched them play, feeling the energy coming off them in waves. There really was no rush now, no urgency. Tongues just fused with chocolate and skin, body parts disappeared into mouths and then appeared again in the golden light of the space. It was a beautiful scene, but it lacked one player. He knew now what he wanted to do, and so he started to walk towards the bathroom.

"Thank you," Dominique said to him, catching him en route.

"A good time was had by all..." Raul said, kissing his wife with familiar passion.

"Yes," she said, looking at Reed licking chocolate from between Sophie's legs. Sophie's fingers moved over Reed and Jeb's erections, sending her own chocolate-covered strawberry into Reed's mouth in waves. They were all three of them on the sofa now, comfortably so because it was so large.

Raul spanked his wife, pushing her towards this trio, encouraging her unnecessarily to join in. He didn't need to tell her twice, Dominique removing Sophie's fingers off Jeb and replacing them with her mouth.

Jeb sat up almost immediately, feeling what was now a familiar mouth on him, remembering what this meant earlier, hoping, knowing that this would mean the same thing now. Sophie wrapped her legs around Reed's head, pulling him to her more, letting go of him with her fingers now so that he could position himself properly for the assignment she had now given him.

Jeb and Dominique were going at it again, Dominique again seated on Jeb, grinding slowly as his thickness disappeared inside her. Her head rested on top of his, the only movement between them coming from her hips. Nothing else was necessary, as they found and maintained a perfect rhythm.

Reed had come up to Sophie's chest with his mouth, pulling in her nipples with his teeth as he too disappeared inside her. Measured thrusts were the order of the day now as he enjoyed the only women he had not yet experienced, realizing as he drove himself into her that everything Jeb had said about her was the absolute truth.

Raul watched for a while, watching Reed especially. He really had a way on a woman, something he hadn't noticed until now. He seemed to be aggressive and not, hard but soft all at once. His confidence wasn't visible, not until he was well and truly in it. Raul knew that Rachel had probably experienced this over and over again during their relationship. He wondered if this was why she assumed control, unable to handle these conflicting sensations, sensations that were working very well on Sophie now, it seemed.

Reed didn't even break a sweat. He seemed to have mastered breathing and control. It was actually incredibly appealing, visually, and Raul made a mental note to apply this technique with Dominique, who seemed spent after she had had Reed inside her. Another mental note Raul made was not to apply it to Rachel, though. It had to be new and interesting. He still didn't know why, but he had the incredible urge to please her.

CHAPTER 9

"PERMISSION TO ENTER..." Raul whispered as he pushed the bathroom door open. Rachel didn't respond, not hearing him, the water inside the large cubicle pouring all over her. She was moving her hands all over herself, the excessive suds of white moving across her flawless skin almost as quickly as the water was washing them away.

He stood in the room watching her through the mist, taking in the splendor. She looked like a model in an ad for shampoo, shower gel, high-end bathroom fittings, *everything*. Raul was rock solid just from the visual. He could have stood there for hours.

Slowly he approached. He wasn't as sure of himself as he would have like to be, but he knew that he probably would never be. He had to just take the plunge, throw himself into it. It was now or never.

He pulled the glass door open and stepped inside. Rachel didn't turn around immediately, although she was aware of the presence in the cubicle. She probably didn't want to see who it was, not wanting to get her hopes up.

Raul put his hand on her head, in her hair, and pulled

her back so that she turned towards him. Her eyes were closed and so he put his lips on her forehead, then on her cheeks. When his mouth met hers, she opened her eyes. Raul was looking at her, looking into her and through her. He smiled even though he was kissing her passionately. She was also smiling, more inside though.

His hands moved over every part of her, touching her with deliberate intent, making her melt into him. His fingers, long and thick, went down between her thighs, touching her with such appreciation that she felt almost vulnerable. She hung on to him from his neck, needing some support, feeling the threat of melting into the floor or disappearing down the drain.

"You're incredibly beautiful," Raul said, before kissing her on her neck, and down her chest. His fingers moved lightly over her, with no threat that they would enter, even though this is all she wanted right now. But he seemed to know what he was doing, what he wanted to do, and so she relaxed into it, trusting that whatever it was, it would be fantastic.

His mouth on her nipples sent fire through her, heat that went all the way to where his fingers played. His other hand was against the small of her back, making it unnecessary for her to hold herself up anymore. He really seemed to have full control of the moment, and she liked it, even though it was a little confusing for her. And Rachel didn't do well with confusion.

Then his finger started to move into her, and all confusion faded. He was telling her with just this finger, no words, that she would have to do absolutely nothing. He was saying, moving this finger in deep circles almost through her, that all he wanted was for her to be here, present with him, now.

She was, of course.

His mouth was back on hers and she was definitely kissing him as much as he was her. Her hands moved through his hair, and then up and down the sides of his broad frame. Then she gripped his firm behind and pulled him towards her, or rather pulled herself into him. Raul's feet were planted firmly into the wet shower floor, solid as a tree. He pulled out his single finger, and then ever so gently, without removing his mouth from her, replaced it with two.

Rachel braced herself on him now, her fingers dug into his sides as he dug his way into her. His fingers were thick, and she was incredibly *resistant*, both of them knowing that this probably had more to do with the fact that she had not yet had an orgasm. Raul got his two fingers all the way up inside her, lingered for a moment, and then slowly removed both. He went in with his long finger now, just the one, and moved it in and out of her, hard and determined, yet beautifully sensual.

He kept at it, kept his mouth on her, willing her closer and closer, rather quickly, to climax. She rippled over the edge unexpectedly, and as she started a mild flow from her love fountain, he added a second finger again, arresting her mid-orgasm, pulling her hair back so that their faces separated and they were once again looking at each other.

She exhaled hard, then took a deep breath as the fingers inside her started to move. The tightness of the wrap intensified every sensation, every movement. The fingers never left her completely once, reaching far into her and then just teasing her with the possibility of exit. She was almost relieved at this possibility, but then he was all the way inside her again.

Confusion took a hold briefly, but this was quickly overtaken by another pending orgasm. This time it was more intense, and she shook as his fingers, just the two thick digits, catapulted her into ecstasy. The build-up was almost as powerful as the actual climax, and Rachel was breathless. Raul too couldn't breathe it seemed, separating his mouth from hers to take in some air. Quickly though his mouth was back on hers as he finished up in her with his middle and index.

He was whispering something in Spanish as he pulled the two fingers from her. Then his mouth was on her chest, on her nipples, down her belly, and then directly on her secret place as he went down on his knees. He held her legs apart, pushed her against the wall, and made a meal out of her dripping center. He was so deliberate, so masterful, that all she could do was put her hands on his head and close her eyes.

Raul brought Rachel to another beautiful climax. His mouth on her, his tongue inside her, everything that was happening to her, that had already happened to her, culminated in the most wonderful euphoria. The series of circumstances worked together so magnificently that she couldn't even think of Raul's pleasure, not now at least. She didn't need to, though, because he had made it exceptionally clear that this was all about her.

CHAPTER 10

RAUL SAT DOWN NOW and lifted Rachel onto him. His shaft in hand, he guided himself into her and she leaned forward, putting both her hands on the glass. To his surprise, he got all the way inside her, facilitated by the fact that she too pushed herself down on him. Raul gripped her hips and started to move her on him in ways that she had never thought were possible.

"You're amazing," he just kept saying, over and over again. She was thinking exactly the same thing, although the words couldn't come out of her mouth.

He wanted to kiss her again, but couldn't. His eyes were glued to where their bodies were fused, *interlocked intimately*. Rachel wasn't moving at all, there was no need to. Raul was in the driver's seat, and although he too wasn't moving except for his hands, he was guiding both of them towards *wonderland*.

Then he let go of her hips and ran his fingers over her breasts. He squeezed her nipples, just the right pressure to send shards of pleasure when he was inside her. He moved just one hand around her neck, the other one busy fingering her nipples. His eyes still glued to where their bodies met, she too looked down now. Her hips were moving now, without her consent. He had gotten her body to go into autopilot, and they both seemed genuinely lost in one another.

He was getting close, but he didn't want this to be over. Not yet. He wanted to stay this way for hours, but he knew this was not possible. Raul looked at her face now and watched as the spray from the shower fell around her and onto his chest. Then he thrust up into her just once before letting her resume her largely involuntary riding of him.

"How did you do that?" she asked, herself incredibly close now.

"We did that," he said, thrusting into her again before pausing.

When her body starting to move over his with increased intensity, he placed his hand on her hip, slowing her down. He was so close and wanted nothing more than to spill himself over into her. But he also wanted to drag this moment out for as long as he possibly could.

He planted his feet into the tiles, and slowly started to bring himself up to standing. He was really incredibly strong, and the ease with which he lifted both of them from the floor was incredible. He turned them around so that her back was against the glass, her body still perched perfectly on his hard place.

She didn't move as he just held her up and fed her every last inch of himself, over and over again. He seemed to have arrested his own need to climax now, but he could do nothing about stopping her own. Rachel was shuddering as again she climaxed, more intense than both previous times.

Raul kept her up, not moving now, determined that his own end wouldn't come just yet. He lifted her off himself and let her feet touch the ground before he turned her to face the glass, her back to him. They both could see through the mist that Reed was standing, watching them. He had probably come in to pee, and couldn't bring himself to leave. He was hard again, pulling on himself, watching the Spaniard take full ownership of his wife.

Raul's eyes stayed on Reed as he found the inside of Rachel again. She inhaled and closed her eyes as he started to thrust into her. Each stroke was full and complete. Each movement of his thick, long shaft was perfect individually but worked incredibly well together. Rachel seemed to be in mad lust now, biting her bottom lip as Raul drove himself into her again and again.

When he pulled out completely she opened her eyes and saw that Reed had moved closer. He stayed on the outside of the glass though, his wife just out of his reach, his throbbing hardness in his own hand. Then Raul was inside her again, and again her eyes closed. He went harder, deeper almost, and she felt again as though she might disappear down the drain.

But Raul's *piller* made sure that she was going nowhere. She stumbled but he held her up, using nothing but the strength of his mast. He sent himself into her harder and harder, but not faster, bringing her up onto her tiptoes with each perfectly executed stroke. She placed her hands against the glass now, holding herself up. Reed reached with his free hand and touched his hand to hers, the only thing between them was the steamed-up pane.

Raul held her hips again, kept her firmly in place now, and started his journey towards the end. It had been everything that he wanted it to be. It had certainly been everything he needed. But Reed really looked like he wanted his wife back now, and so he had to bring this magical moment to its end. He really didn't want to still, but such were the rules of this game.

His pace didn't change still, though. His intensity was another story completely. It felt, to Rachel at least, that the man inside her had grown in length and girth. He was pushing against every part of her now, threatening to bring her to yet another orgasm. When he made good in this threat, Reed and Rachel both could not believe it. Reed's disbelief stemmed from a whole other place, however.

When Raul finally tripped over the edge, he seemed to be caught in a trance. It was only when Reed finally pulled the glass door open that he eventually slid himself out of Rachel, thanking both of them before leaving the bathroom and going to find his senses and his wife...

ABOUT THE AUTHOR

Tena Seldan is an emerging erotica author of many erotica kinks and sub-genres. Be sure to check out other books and leave a review if this story got you hot!

Visit my blog at Tena Seldan Blog

Join my newsletter for exclusive previews
Tena Seldan Newsletter

Sign up for Free Stories from Xplicit Press Authors
Xplicit Press Author Updates
Like Xplicit Press on Facebook
Follow Xplicit Press on Twitter

Readers: I want to expand a few of the stories to see where the characters can be explored further. If there are any of the stories that you would like to read more about again, I'd love to hear from you!

Keep In Touch
Tena Seldan
info@tenaseldan.com